Erotic Stories for Women

Bad Boys Billionaire

Rough Erotica Short Stories

Vivienne Dupont

Table of Contents

The Millionaire - Seduced by the Boss

I take a deep breath as I stand in front of the huge building that I will be visiting every day starting today. At least during the week.

"Good morning," I hear a man mutter as he pushes past me to go through the swinging door.

"Hello," I reply uncertainly and have to collect myself once again. I have only recently completed my studies. Actually, I had planned to travel a bit afterwards to Asia and Australia - but then came the job offer and changed my plans. It was an offer I couldn't possibly refuse. After all, this is not just any company, but one of the best in town. My boss is none other than Jackson Harvey, a real megastar in his industry, despite the fact that he's only 32. And although I probably won't be working with him anyway, I was drawn in by the temptation to work *for him.*

"Are you going to stand in the way any longer?" the man at the front desk calls out to me, who must have been watching me avoid going in for ten minutes already.

"Oh," I mutter, embarrassed, and step inside.

"First day?" he asks me, to which I nod eagerly. "Well, tell me your name first, and then we'll see."

Relieved, I exhale. "Okay."

"You don't have to be nervous. I see you're starting in the press department? They're all very nice and easygoing. And if you've managed to convince Jane of your worth, then you certainly have your credentials to be here," he says, addressing my new boss.

"Is she that ... picky?", I ask.

Eagerly, he nods. "Oh, yes. Very."

At the moment, I feel a little better. That's something.

I take my new key card and drive up to the 5th floor. Just as Simon, the man at the front desk, wrote it down for me.

Confused, I look around when I arrive on the floor. "Excuse me?" I address a woman who is walking past me under stress. Annoyed, she rolls her eyes, but remains standing.

"The press department? Where can I find it?"

Wordlessly, she points to an office in the corner and then hurries on.

I take a look at the clock. Whew. I am still much too late due to my dawdling. So I don't think twice and hurry toward the closed door, which I now swing open.

Suddenly, five pairs of eyes turn in my direction and look at me in shock as I stand in the doorway. "Hi, I'm the new girl. Diane," I introduce myself and wave carefully.

I recognise Jane and walk towards her, but she pretends to see me for the first time today and continues to just stare at me. Finally she seems to remember me again and that yes I am starting today, which is why she slowly walks towards me. "Oh sorry. I completely forgot about you. It's all over the place here today." She points to the handsome man in the black suit who is staring intently at a photo. He looks suspiciously like the CEO.

"There's a rumour doing the rounds at the moment," she tells me. "It could end pretty badly if it turns out to be true. That's why we're all working flat out right now. Actually, it's quite good that you're starting this week of all weeks. It gives us one more helping hand."

She shows me my desk and lets me in on it, then goes back to her work.

I sit haphazardly in front of my computer and first familiarise myself with my new work environment before turning to my colleague from the neighbouring table.

"Sorry. The scandal. What's that about?" I whisper to her.

Skeptically, she looks at me before deciding to tell me everything. "It's about Mr. Dwight. He's been on the board for years. And now he's being accused of having an affair with a minor."

"Oh my," I mutter.

"We are now trying everything to avert the scandal as far as possible, or at least to keep it small enough not to damage the business."

"Mm?", I say, aware to keep quiet so I can hear more of the details.

"I'm pretty sure it's already leaked and I think all we can do now is damage control. But no one knows with what." With that, she turns away again, leaving me alone with my thoughts.

I have no idea how to help and look around for Jane, hoping that she might give me a specific task, but she seems to be very busy.

So I try to find out more about this Mr. Dwight and spend my first day of work doing that without really doing anything.

"Oh, Diane?", Jane stops me just before I disappear into closing time. "I didn't even have time to look at your results today. Tomorrow we can talk about it, right? I've seen how hard you've researched. I'm excited to see what you've come up with."

Without me even being able to say anything back, she disappears again and dismisses me with a guilty conscience. Oh dear.

I hurry home, where I run into my roommate Olive, who immediately wants to know how my first day at work went. I tell her about the scandal and that my new boss wants to see results tomorrow.

"And what results do you have?" she asks.

"Well, none. I know Mr. Dwight's complete resume. Know how many children he has, who his wife is, etc. But that's about it."

"Mh," she makes and tries to figure out with me how to proceed.

"Children he has, you say?"

"Yes, a son and a daughter."

"And how old is this son?"

"He's still in school. I think around 17 or 18."

"Perfect!"

"Why perfect?"

"Well, show me a picture of him."

I pull out my phone and show her the family photo I found of the Dwights.

"Looks a lot like his dad, doesn't he? The spitting image of him."

"It's possible. But why does it matter?"

"Well ... we had something similar once. Affair with someone much younger. We reenacted photos. With his son and the girl. Made it look like they'd always been a couple and the informant just confused son with father."

"Like that's going to work."

"It's worth a try, isn't it?"

"Mm." Once again, I look at the photo. Yes, it might be worth a try.

I go further into the kitchen and warm up the leftovers from yesterday, before I let the evening end in front of the TV.

When I arrive at the office the next morning, everyone is running around stressed out.

"Ah, Diana! You're the one I've been waiting for," Jane says, coming toward me. "Please tell me you found something useful."

I immediately dig out my cell phone and show her the photo. Then I submit to her the proposal that Olive made to me.

"Whew ... so maybe that could actually work," she says, "Come on. We'll go up to see Mr. Harvey. We'll see what he has to say about it."

"To Mr. Harvey?", I say nervously.

"Yes, yes. He's very interested in getting this sorted out quickly." She walks ahead and I follow.

As we stand in the elevator, I glance uncertainly at the mirrored wall. Last night, Olive explained to me at length why she is so jealous of my new job.

"This Mr. Harvey is a real treat. If I had him as a boss ... phew. I wouldn't be able to concentrate on work at all," she kept muttering. But I kept shaking my head at that. "I have nothing to do with him. He's up on his executive floor and I'm at the bottom. We never see each other."

But now I'm on my way to meet him and I'm supposed to tell him about my proposal. All of a sudden my heart is beating like crazy and my hands are getting all wet.

"Celine, we need to get to Jackson," I hear Jane say to a blonde woman, who then points to the locked door.

"He's still on the phone. Wait a minute, please. I'll let him know." She directs us to the sofa and nervously I take a seat there. Olive even showed me some magazine clippings of him yesterday, which don't necessarily make the whole situation any better right now. Because, what I read and saw there ... phew.

"He's ready," I hear the blonde woman say, whereupon Jane immediately jumps up and looks at me expectantly.

"Are you coming?"

"Yeah," I mumble, suddenly feeling like I'm another student who's done something wrong and is now on her way to the principal's office.

"Hey Jane," he greets us, giving me a confused look when he sees me trotting into his office behind Jane. "And you are?" he asks me, coming toward me.

Oh God. With his whole 1.91m he stands in front of me. His tart perfume rises in my nose and I can literally feel the dominance he radiates.

"This is Diane, my newest employee," Jane introduces me when I don't respond.

Oh man. This man does something to me that I can't explain. He unsettles me.

"I hope she's here for a good reason," he says, turning to Jane.

"Tell him about your plan," she now turns to me.

Awkwardly, I stand in the middle of the room and don't know what to do with myself. So I start and give Olive's suggestion for the second time.

"Mm ... maybe this really is our only chance," Mr. Harvey muses aloud. "We could give it a try. Can you take care of it?" he now asks me. "And if there's any news, please report back to me immediately, will you?"

"Yes," I murmur softly and look into Jane's satisfied face, who then pulls me out of his office.

"Well, that went well. I know, he can be very intimidating at first, but if you do a good job, you have nothing to fear from him." Encouragingly, she pats me on the shoulder as we get into the elevator.

Once downstairs, she leaves me alone again. How the hell am I supposed to accomplish this task to satisfy him?

I immediately sit down at the desk and start researching. Find out where the son goes to school. I make contact with the girl. I arrange a meeting for the next day and hope that the scandal will vanish into thin air.

"Mr. Harvey asks when you'll finally deliver results," I hear Jane ask me the next day. "Soon," I reply, looking into her stern face.

"Listen, this is really important, okay? Please take this a little more seriously."

I think about this scandal around the clock. I couldn't take it any more seriously if I tried!

"Come on, show me what you already have. I'm getting calls nonstop so I can give them an update up there." She comes up to me and looks over my shoulders. I show her the pictures of Mr. Dwight's nephew. "Mm. That could really work. When are you meeting him?"

"Today," I reply immediately.

"Good." With that, she leaves me alone again.

I have the appointment confirmed once again and take one of the photographers from the house with me to recreate the photos. We need almost the entire morning to be reasonably satisfied. But if you squint your eyes really hard, it might actually work.

"It's our only chance," I sigh aloud as we arrive back at the office and I say goodbye to the photographer.

He wishes me good luck and gives me a print of the photos to show Mr. Harvey.

When I open the door to the office, I look directly at my colleague Nicole, who is sitting crying at her desk. I look around. Jane has disappeared. "What's going on?" I want to know.

"She was fired," a colleague tells me, unimpressed.

"What?!"

"From the boss himself."

"From Mr. Harvey?"

"Yes."

"But why?", I ask in a panic.

"She didn't do her job properly."

Jesus. I can feel my hands getting wet. Now I'm even more afraid to show him the result. What if he's not happy with it?

"Where's Jane?", I ask cautiously, checking with her first.

"Not there," is the curt reply. "But I'm supposed to tell you to show the photos directly to Mr. Harvey when you get back."

Oh God. Now I have to go in there alone?!

My heart is pounding as I get back into the elevator and head upstairs.

"Mr. Harvey is not in right now. Can you stay until he gets back?" his assistant asks me.

I nod and am even a bit relieved. Now I have a little more grace period. I arrange with her to call me when he's back and go back to the others, where chaos still reigns. But I try to concentrate and think of the words for my meeting with Mr. Harvey.

It's getting later and later, and so far there's been no call. The rest of my colleagues have long since left the office as I sit lonely and alone in the room, clicking away on my computer. I have no task left and start reading any articles from the day. My stomach is growling and I drank the last of my water some time ago. So I decide to get up and go to the small office kitchen to make myself some more tea.

When I return with the hot cup in my hand, suddenly someone is sitting on Jane's chair. I almost drop the tea from my hand in shock when I realise who it is: Mr. Harvey.

"There you are," he greets me, looking at me sternly. "I thought you'd just disappeared. I specifically told you to wait."

I wince. What stern words. He made me wait here for so long. Who asks their employees to be here three hours after closing time? "Sorry," I mumble, setting my cup down on the desk. Then I dig out the photo and wordlessly shove it into his hand.

"Mm," he murmurs, narrowing his eyes to two slits. "And that's all you've got?"

Again I flinch..that's all? It's taken us the whole morning. "Yes," I reply somewhat meekly.

"Mh," he mouths again and looks at the photo once more. "So if we edit it a bit more, then it might work out altogether." He puts the photo away again and looks at me expectantly. "So what's next? How do you want to proceed?"

I tell him about the further plan, whereupon he merely nods.

"I think this is our only chance." He doesn't seem very enthusiastic. "Very well. Let's leave it for today. Let's continue tomorrow." With those words, he gets up and just leaves me alone.

What?! Continue tomorrow? With what? What else does he expect! I'm getting a headache just thinking that tomorrow I'll have to wait for him for another 3 hours for a 5 minute conversation.

As if petrified, I remain sitting on my chair until my stomach finally makes itself known. It growls. So I pack up and leave.

At home, I tell Olive about the incident, who merely looks at me in awe.

"He's really scary, isn't he?"

"Oh, yes," I agree.

"Scary, but also hot. Yes?"

Annoyed, I roll my eyes. I didn't pay attention to whether he was hot, too, while he was making me a slug. But she always lives in her own world anyway.

"How did it go yesterday with Mr. Harvey?" Jane wants to know when I come into the office the next morning. I tell her about the evening and she gives me a stern look.

"Well, then you know what you have to do today."

I look at her questioningly. No, what? I don't know what else to tell him. But then a colleague turns to me and helps me to prepare something. And indeed, it looks like the posed photo will come in handy and we can avert the scandal.

I don't hear anything from him or his assistant all day, and when everyone goes home in the evening, I remain seated.

"Mr. Harvey wanted to see me later today," I explain to Jane as she looks at me questioningly.

"Oh yeah, that's right. I should tell you that it might be a little late," she says simply as she puts on a jacket.

Great. So I stay seated and wait.

Again my stomach growls. I could have really learned from yesterday and packed myself some more food, but who could have expected that he would make me wait so long twice?

Just as I'm about to get up and go to the bathroom, the door opens.

"Hello," he says busily and comes into the office without hesitation. "Tell me quickly, what's new."

So I tell him about the developments and that it looks like the scandal will indeed blow over soon.

"Whew," he says with relief, leaning back in his chair. "This has really been on my mind the last couple of days. I've been really tense."

I feel not only his tension but also mine slowly falling away from me.

Now he even starts to smile. "God, I must have been obnoxious. Forgive me. But this is good news. Really good."

I now force myself to smile as well and notice how the ice between us has broken.

Suddenly my stomach growls again. So loud that even he can't miss it. He glances at the clock. "Oh dear. So late already. I'm sorry. I must have totally delayed you."

He did, yes. But I would never admit that. "It's okay."

He thinks for a moment and then looks at me questioningly. "Do you like sushi?"

Irritated, I raise an eyebrow. "Yes...", I answer more questioningly.

"For the meeting earlier, we ordered lots of sushi. There should still be some left. If you want, we can go up and grab the leftovers," he suggests.

I do not answer. Instead, my stomach does, because it growls again unmistakably.

Mr. Harvey laughs, then stands up. "Let's go."

Shyly, I go after him and together we enter the elevator that is supposed to take us upstairs. We stand opposite each other and I notice that he is looking at me attentively. When I look at him, he just grins cheekily. "Be right there," he says innocently and gives me his irresistible smile again.

If I told Olive about this, she would freak out!

We arrive upstairs and he leads me into the small kitchen. Immediately he tears open the refrigerator and pulls out the plastic boxes. "It's all still there."

I take a pair of chopsticks and reach for one of the boxes. Uncertainly, I stop. Was this an invitation to eat with him up here or did he just want to give me the leftovers and then send me home with them?

"What are you waiting for? Eat!" he replies, as if he had just read my thoughts.

I pull one of the chairs out from under the table and drop onto it. He sits down opposite me.

Silently, we tuck into the sushi. The mood is strange. I daren't say anything, but at the same time I can't stand the silence.

"So, tell me," he suddenly starts. "How long have you been working here?" he wants to know.

"Just a few days," I reply and have to stifle a smile. He must have thought I'd been working here for years.

"Oh!" Again he muses at me. "Well, what a debut! But I can reassure you. Things aren't usually that stressful here. This was just an exceptional situation."

"Well, I'm reassured."

We start chatting. About my studies, my previous part-time jobs and what I expect from this position.

Mr. Harvey is unusually nice. I really didn't expect that at first. We get along well. He's funny and interesting, he listens attentively at the same time and asks questions in the right places. If this were a date, and that's what it feels like right now, I'd chalk it up as a complete success.

But he is my boss and I am just an employee.

By now we've eaten almost all of the sushi and I can feel the rice expanding in my stomach.

"I can't eat anymore," I say, pushing the last pieces away from me.

"You're full?" he asks.

"Oh yeah."

"Fine." He looks at his wristwatch. "It's getting late, too. I won't keep you any longer."

"Oh, you didn't," I contradict him. After all, I really enjoyed the last hour with him.

He smiles and this time I even dare to withstand his intense gaze. Something is happening between us right now. "I'm glad," he answers after a long pause.

He gets up and suddenly stands close to me.

I daren't move. He comes closer. I can smell his tangy scent.

He looks down at me, reaches out and touches me gently on my cheek.

Oh, God, what's happening?

He touches me on my shoulder and finally reaches for my arm, by which he now pulls me up to him.

I look into his face. Into his flawless face with his blue eyes that continue to look intensely. Then he licks his tongue over his lips, moistens them and then opens his mouth slightly.

20

I look at his full, curved lips and slowly lean forward.

We kiss each other. Very carefully and gently.

But it doesn't stop there. The kiss becomes more passionate, more demanding and before I know it, I'm sitting on the kitchen counter, spreading my legs and have him between them.

He grabs me, touches me everywhere with his hands until they finally stray between my legs. He pushes up my skirt and touches the delicate fabric of my panties with his fingers.

I moan out loud when I feel his touch, which makes my entire body quiver. Again we kiss. My hands bury themselves in his hair. I want to feel him as close to me as possible.

"Oh God, you're wet," he suddenly whispers in my ear as he pushes the fabric of my panties aside and slides his fingertip through my cleft. "Mh," he moans as he lets two fingers sink deep inside me.

I also moan. Enjoy this hard movement and how he fucks me hard with his two fingers. God!

He takes his hand away again and pushes my panties off my hips. Then he spreads my legs again and looks greedily at my naked pussy. Then he bends down, licks with his tongue over my wet cleft, and then kisses me again.

My smell on his chin makes me completely insane!

I start to undress him. Strip his jacket from his shoulders, open his shirt and finally his pants.

His bulging cock jumps out at me and I start massaging it with my hand.

Again he grabs me. Pulls me closer to him by the legs, so that I am only half sitting on the counter. He reaches for his cock and now puts it to my pussy. With one hand he holds my shoulder and then penetrates me.

Oh man. That feels so good. He starts fucking me. Hard and fast.

He interrupts briefly. Pulls me off the counter and turns me around. My upper body now lies on the cold, smooth surface, while his hand wanders over my ass and gives him a little slap.

I moan lustfully while he now pushes his spanking deep inside me again and fucks me once more.

My hands hold onto the counter with all their might as he presses me harder and harder against it.

All you can hear is the slapping of skin against skin and our loud groans.

He speeds up, then slows down again. I can feel him enjoying it.

Then he grabs me again. Pushes me to the floor. I kneel in front of him. His cock directly in front of my face. Begging I open my mouth and grinning he pushes his spanking into my mouth, which I now blow with relish.

He comes to rest. His hands are on my head and on my shoulder. He closes his eyes and enjoys my tongue on his cock.

"Oh God, you're doing so well," he moans, suddenly pulling me back up.

Determined, he pushes me over the table where we just ate. My face lands just next to the soy sauce and again his cock pushes into my pussy.

I feel everything inside me contracting. How my body begins to tense up. I'm about to come.

His thrusts become harder. His panting louder. He too is about to come.

"I'll be right there," I press out, digging my fingers into the tabletop.

"Yeah, come for me," he mumbles and continues to thrust hard.

And then it happens. A violent orgasm brews in me and I come.

Trembling, I remain lying on the table while he pushes hard into me a few more times and then climaxes as well.

I feel him twitch. I hear him take a deep breath and pause.

Very slowly, he pulls back. And I also straighten up again.

Grinning, we look at each other.

"So this ..." he starts and smiles.

"...was not planned," I finish his sentence, whereupon he nods.

"Exactly."

"Spontaneous things are the best anyway."

"That's right."

We get dressed again, clean up the mess we just made, and head back downstairs.

"So," we say as we stand in the entryway. "Do you still want me to take you home?" he asks me.

"No, it's all right," I decline, thinking of my bike, which is parked at the stop.

"Okay. Then I guess I'll see you tomorrow," he says goodbye and gives me his irresistible smile once again.

"Right. See you tomorrow."

I turn around and disappear in the direction of the subway.

Oh man. I really didn't expect this outcome and can't wait to tackle the next project.

You belong to me

"*Destiny is calling me. Open up my eager eyes. 'Cause I'm Mr. Brightside,*" I sing out loud as I mop the hallway floor. Once again I dip the mop into the dirty cleaning water and let it clap loudly on the tiles. Just this room and I'm finally done with this overly large house that my boss, Mr. Gilmore, occupies completely alone.

I take a look at the clock. Almost 6 p.m. It took me a really long time today. It's always like this on Mondays. Because I don't come over on weekends because he's usually here then and doesn't like it when I clean in his presence. And I don't like him looking over my shoulder while I'm cleaning.

Plus, he always likes to host guys' nights on the weekends, which end up getting pretty out of hand. That's why I always have so much to do on Mondays.

Exhausted, I empty the bucket in the toilet and stow the cleaning utensils in the closet. Tomorrow I'll continue with dusting.

I hang my apron on the hook on the inside of the door and close the closet again. Mr. Gilmore will be home in the next half hour so I should be on my way.

Once again I check that everything is really clean and that I have also put everything back before I sneak out the back door. Once I dared to leave a cleaning cloth behind. The fuss was huge. Mr. Gilmore can be a real asshole at times and most of all, very scary. I genuinely wonder now and then what dramas he's already been through in his life to be *like that*. But at least he pays very well and if I stick to the rules and make sure not to leave anything lying around, everything is great. Then I can also loudly bawl my favourite song without anyone noticing anything.

A few days later, I return to Mr. Gilmore's house and am surprised to see his car still parked in the driveway. I had checked the time when I left earlier. He should have been in the office by now.

"Hello?", I call cautiously into the house as I unlock it with my key.

"Miranda, I'm here," echoes through the hallway.

I frown in confusion. Is that Ben, the gardener, already? Wasn't he supposed to come tomorrow? I follow the voice and almost trip when I suddenly see him, Mr. Gilmore himself, sitting in the kitchen.

"You?" I say in shock, looking up into his stern face. I haven't run into my boss very often. Every day I admire the photos with his family on the mantel, but in person I've only seen him at the job interview and the few times we've met here at the house.

"Yes, feel free to come closer," he prompts me.

Carefully, I put one step in front of the other. I go through the last few days. Did I leave a rag somewhere after all? Was the floor too slippery last time? Should I clean them first next time? Jesus. Is he trying to tell me I'm fired? But I need the job!

"Yes?" I say uncertainly, looking at the smile that has formed on his face. What's going on here!

"Why are you so afraid of me?" he asks with amusement, his blue eyes twinkling.

Oh, God. He's got me. "I ... uh," I stammer, barely able to meet his gaze. There's something about him that unnerves the hell out of me. And I can't even tell what.

Yes, he is attractive. Very attractive, even. But at the same time, there's something dark, almost sinister about him that has always ensured that I didn't see him as the attractive millionaire, but only as the stern boss who might also have been in a perfume ad by chance.

"That's okay. You don't have to answer that," he cuts me off and I exhale in relief. I wouldn't have had an answer anyway. "I got the news last night that I can do my next project from home, too. I've been travelling a lot the last few weeks and have hardly been home. So I jumped at the chance and said yes to the proposal."

I stare at him with wide eyes. Is he trying to tell me that he's home during every one of my shifts?

"That means we'll have to share space in the house during the day," he voices my thoughts. "But don't worry, you won't even notice I'm here. I'll adjourn to my office." He gives me a friendly smile and then turns on the counter stool to the side to jump down and leave me alone.

I stop in the kitchen, flabbergasted. What was that just now?! Why was he so friendly?

Irritated, I stow my bag at the coat rack and get to work. Mr. Gilmore is right. I don't even notice that he's there. So everything stays the same.

After just under a week, I have completely forgotten that I am no longer alone in the house. It's a terribly muggy August day when I park my car in front of the house and head off to work more scantily clad than usual. But the skimpy clothing doesn't help. I'm sweating like a fool as I'm cleaning the windows and have to constantly wipe the sweat from my forehead with the palm of my hand.

"Whew," I exhale loudly and have to straighten my wireless headphones for the umpteenth time because they keep coming loose or off due to sweat. I always listen to music at work. It helps me concentrate much better. For a brief moment, I consider getting rid of my T-shirt as well. Today I wear a sports bra underneath. It could also pass for a top. When I touch my back and notice how the T-shirt is soaked with sweat, I pull it over my head and lay it on the terrace to dry. No one will see me. Especially not Mr. Gilmore, who is quietly working away in his office.

I turn my attention back to the windows and make my way through the house. I climb the stairs and continue in the guest room. I turn the music up a bit louder while I carefully clean window after window.

In a good mood, I hum along to my favourite song until I see a figure in the doorway out of the corner of my eye. Oh God!

I quickly turn around and stand rooted to the spot. It's Mr. Gilmore, who is watching me with amusement as I clean the windows half-naked while singing.

I take the headphones out of my ears and just stare at him. For a change, he's not wearing a suit, but just a pair of shorts. His upper body shines with sweat and the sight of him almost drives me crazy.

"It's really hot today, isn't it?" he asks, eyeing me.

I instantly realise that I'm no longer wearing a top and try to cover myself with the rag. But it is useless, he has already seen me.

"The air conditioner was supposed to be repaired weeks ago. But unfortunately, the repair companies are hopelessly booked up. Surely I'll have cool rooms again in the winter." He smiles and takes a step toward me. "Phew, you're all sweaty. I'm sorry to hear that. I should make for a pleasant working atmosphere."

I don't know what to say to that. The heat is absolutely no problem for me. "Um. That's okay," I stammer again, cursing myself at the same time. Why am I so insecure in his presence?

"I was going to take a quick dip in the pool. Won't you come with me?"

In the pool? With him? Is he serious? "Um," I merely do, shaking my head. "No, thank you."

"Oh, don't make such a fuss. I won't tell your boss either," now he winks too. Help?!

Hesitantly, I nod. How can I say no to him?! To this face and to my boss, who usually doesn't accept back talk. In the end, it's all planned just to look for a reason to get rid of me.

"But I didn't bring any bathing suits," I say as I carefully follow him up the stairs.

"Wait a minute," he says simply, and turns around again to open the closet in the upstairs hallway. It reveals lots of towels and a box of swim trunks and bikinis.

"My friends like to forget their bathing suits here. Probably on purpose so they can get right into the pool the next time they visit. Take your pick."

Overwhelmed, I look into the box, where a large amount of skimpy bikinis are. I am more the type of sporty swimsuit. Now and then it may also be a two-piece, but then it consists of wide shoulder straps and is not only held together with thin threads.

"This one looks appropriate, doesn't it," he rushes to my aid and selects the skimpiest piece.

"You sure?" I ask uncertainly, to which he nods eagerly.

"This will look excellent on you."

I retreat to the bathroom and peel myself out of my soaking wet clothes. Then I slip into the bikini and retie the bows at my hips and neck so that it fits better.

Cautiously, I take a look in the mirror. It fits, yes. But the sight is unusual. I don't usually show myself in such a ... revealing way.

I shyly emerge from the bathroom again and face Mr. Gilmore's critical gaze, but he just grins. "Told you. Fits great." With that, he turns back to the stairs and walks slowly down them.

I follow him and a little later we find ourselves at the large pool in the garden.

How often I have dreamed of jumping in here one day. During my hours here, I often imagined myself jumping in uninhibited. But far too great was the fear that Mr. Gilmore would return from work earlier than planned and catch me at it. He would certainly have been upset and fired me.

And yet he is now standing in front of me and inviting me to follow him into the cool water. What on earth is wrong with him?

Hesitantly, I dip the tip of my foot into the water, which has the perfect temperature for today. Not too cold, but not too warm either.

"What better way to cool off on a hot day than in the on-site pool?" he says, flipping onto his back to float on the water's surface.

"To be rich enough to afford an in-home pool," I murmur softly.

"Pardon?" he asks.

"Oh, nothing. That's okay," I wave it off.

"Something about being rich enough to afford a pool? Do I hear envy?"

Of course I am envious. Of him, his money and his lifestyle. I see the remnants of the debauched parties he throws every weekend. The expensive sushi they order and the expensive alcohol they drink. It must be great to be so rich and have no worries at all. "Maybe a little," I openly admit, completely submerging my body under water. Mh ... how good this little cooling off does.

"I know most of the time it looks like my life is all luxuries and parties. But actually, most of the time I'm just stressed out!"

"Oh yes?", I ask.

"A company like this doesn't run itself. I'm under enormous pressure and have to make important decisions on a continuous basis. If I make rash decisions or don't allow myself to go full throttle for even one day, it can cause everything to collapse."

"Oh," is all I say, and I can't even imagine what it's like to be in such a position. If I act rashly, then at most it leads to me having to clean a spot twice.

"Well," he turns back on his stomach and takes a lane. "Anyway, I'm glad when I can switch off a bit in between. Especially, after ...", he pauses and looks up at the sky.

"Especially after?", I ask boldly.

"It's okay." He forces a smile and looks at me. "Let's forget about it."

But I can't forget it. What did he mean by that?

It remains with a small refreshment. Because he is interrupted by an important call and I also have to get back to work to finish again today.

Without a word, he retreats back to his office and I head back upstairs to the nearest windows.

When I leave work in the evening and walk through the hallway, the light in his office is still on. Loud voices push through the closed door. He still seems to be on the phone. So I steal out of the house secretly and go home.

He seems to be away for the next few days, because I don't see him. Which I find almost a bit of a pity. I thought we were slowly getting closer. Because it would make my job a lot easier if I had the feeling that my boss likes me and is satisfied with my work. I never had that before.

Just as I'm about to dust off the pictures in the living room, I hear a door slam. It's Mr. Gilmore, who drops his suitcases loudly on the floor.

Confidently, he marches into the living room and settles down on a sofa. "Oh," he says when he sees me in the corner with the duster. "I didn't know you were here," he replies to me unemotionally. He stands back up and goes to his little bar cart to pour himself a drink. He seems changed. Where is the nice man who invited me to swim in his pool the other day?

"I'm having a little party tomorrow night. Are you free then?"

What? Is he inviting me to a party? No. Impossible. "I am. What can I do for you?"

"Oh ... I'd just need someone to help the bartender out a little bit. You know. He'd mix the drinks and then you'd be in charge of the dishes and a few appetisers. Mainly also making sure I don't wake up to a mess the next morning."

That sounds like a lot of stress, but since my car broke down a few days ago and needs to go to the shop, it also sounds like a good way to earn money for repairs.

"I'll pay you very generously, don't worry," he says after I hesitate a bit.

"All right. I'm free to help."

"Wonderful." He gives me a smile before draining the glass in one go. "I need to make a phone call. If you could please take care of my luggage," he says, then turns away from me. "And after that, please take the rest of the day off. Then tomorrow, please come here at 7 pm. The first guests will arrive at 8 p.m."

I nod, put the duster aside and start to take care of his luggage.

When I'm standing in front of the front door at 7 p.m. on the dot the next day, I almost regret that I said yes. I had a lot to do the rest of the day and actually planned to give myself some time off tonight. But when the dear money calls ...

"Ah, wonderful," I hear Mr. Gilmore say as I stand in the hallway a bit haphazardly, not knowing what to start with.

"Ted has already started setting up the bar. Why don't you give him a hand? And Miranda," he looks me up and down once and raises an eyebrow critically. "It would be nice if the employees wear uniform today. I've already put Ted's uniform out, and yours is waiting for you in the guest room."

My uniform? Couldn't he have told me that earlier? Then I could have saved myself the hour in front of the closet earlier, thinking about what to wear. In the end it became the black jeans with the black T-shirt. Inconspicuous as always.

I walk up to the bartender and get the glasses out of the boxes to line them up on the counter. When we're done with that, I go to the guest room to change.

I close the door behind me and see my uniform on a hanger. A short black skirt and a white blouse. I would have had that at home, too. I take a look at the label. Above all, I would have had something at home that would also fit me. This one seems a size too small. Nevertheless, I put it on. The skirt is actually a little too tight and a little too short. I barely get the top of the blouse closed over my breasts and before a button pops off, I prefer to leave that open. It fits, even if it looks a bit obscene. But I have no more time. The first guests are about to arrive.

I go to the kitchen and prepare a few of the plates and stock them with appetisers from the caterer. When the doorbell rings, I quickly go to the door and open it.

I look in amazement at the three men in suits standing in front of me. I have no idea what I imagined a "small party" to be. I was probably thinking of the parties I've already attended. Casual get-togethers with friends, that is. This one, however, doesn't seem so casual.

"Good evening," they say, looking down at me with interest. I invite them in and discover Mr. Gilmore receiving his guests.

The doorbell rings again and once more I open the door to men in suits, until in the end just under 20 of them have gathered in the spacious living room and are sipping their drinks.

Confused, I look around. Is this a business meeting? Where are the women?

"Miranda," Mr. Gilmore suddenly snaps me out of my thoughts.

Wide-eyed, I stare at him. "Yes?"

"Please take good care of my guests, will you? There are some important business partners with them. Read their every wish from their eyes, okay?"

"All right," I murmur and hope that my tip for this evening will at least be generous. Because normally serving guests is not one of my tasks.

So I rush to the kitchen, put a few more appetisers on the silver trays and run through the crowd with them.

By now, each of them has already had a drink or two and the whole group is a bit more loosened up. To my chagrin. Because as time goes by, they all become a bit more intrusive. Which is possibly also due to the skimpy outfit.

"Can you stay?" Mr. Gilmore asks me at one point. His cheeks are flushed. His drunken grin no longer disappears from his face.

I glance at the clock. "It's already late. Will you need me much longer?" I ask. Actually, I'm not exhausted, just the men are all starting to get on my nerves.

"Oh, we've just started. But if you're tired..."

"Tired no, but ...," I pause and move a little closer as I notice that two of his guests are within earshot. "They're getting pushy." Cautiously, I point in the direction of the crowd.

"You've got to be kidding me!" he huffs, glancing around. "Has anyone touched you indecently yet, too?"

"No, no."

"Fine, I'll make it clear to them that you are mine and not available."

What?! Confused, I look at him.

"Oh, you know. You're my maid. If anyone is allowed to touch you indecently, it's only me," he babbles on. He seems pretty drunk, so I let him get away with it. Sober, he would certainly never have said something like that.

"So? Are you staying?"

"Yeah, okay," I reply, looking up into his face, which now has an even wider grin on it.

"Fine. And if you're tired of serving appetisers, feel free to join us in a toast and celebration." He turns away and greets the two men behind him warmly.

I think about his words. I belong to him and am not available to the others. Did he mean it? Does he really think so?

I lift the next tray and go back into the living room, where the men are rushing straight for the food. In the meantime, music is playing. It is loud and I think that even more guests have followed. It's crowded and now even a few more women have arrived, which relieves me. So at least the attention is not completely on me.

"Hey, wait a minute!" someone yells after me, holding me by the arm.

When I turn around, there's a middle-aged man standing there with his head all red. "Don't you want to drink with us?" he asks, looking unabashedly into my cleavage.

"No, thank you," I murmur and want to stand away. But he does not let go of me.

"Oh, come on sweetie. Why not? The evening is still young and you don't have to carry this tray around all the time. I'm sure your boss won't mind." He pulls me to him and wants to put his arm around my waist.

I resist, push myself away from him, whereupon he gets angry.

"What are you doing? Why are you resisting like this? Ah, do you need money? Do you want me to give you money?"

I look at him in shock. Money for what? That I let him grope me? What does he think?!

"What's going on here?" a strong, familiar voice suddenly interrupts us.

We turn around and behind me is Mr. Gilmore, who stands threateningly in front of the man. "Are you harassing my employee?" he asks.

"No, I ...," he lets go of me and raises his hands apologetically. "I didn't do anything. Honest."

"Is that true?" he looks at me scrutinizingly.

"Um," I murmur, rubbing the spot where the man pulled me a moment ago.

Mr. Gilmore penetrates me with his gaze. He seems really upset. "Nothing happened," I say, so as not to make a big deal out of this.

"Are you sure?" he follows up, continuing to look at me.

"Yeah. Sure."

You can clearly see the tension in his body release. "Okay. Good."

Then he moves on. I quickly move in the other direction and take refuge in the kitchen.

I can't go home yet. Not after he asks me if everything is okay and I agreed to stay earlier. So I carry on as if nothing has happened.

In fact, the incident remains unique. I can still see the man leaving the party accompanied by two men who have to support him and breathe a sigh of relief.

"Are you still working?" I am asked from the side. I turn around and a tall, attractive man is standing next to me. He seems completely sober and smiles at me.

"Yes. After all, the party is still in full swing."

"Your boss is pretty strict, isn't he?"

"Oh, he'll be fine."

"No, no. I know how bossy he can be sometimes. Everyone in the office fears him."

I start to laugh. The man introduces himself to me as Harvey and convinces me to have a drink with him. We talk and suddenly I have a really nice evening. The incident from earlier fades completely into the background.

"What's going on here?" we are interrupted at some point. I clearly recognize the loud voice of Mr. Gilmore.

"Paul. It's nothing," Harvey replies, smiling soothingly at him.

"Yes, it is, you're making a pass at my maid. I can see that." Again, he seems upset. What's wrong with him? Just making conversation.

"We're just talking," Harvey tells him gently.

"Talking. I get it. I can see you staring at them."

I feel like I'm in a fake movie here.

"Calm down, man," Harvey now retorts, but Mr. Gilmore looks increasingly tense.

"Leave her alone, all right? She's mine, okay?!"

There. Those words again. What is he thinking?

"Do you actually hear what you're saying? She is not your property."

The two exchange intense glances while I just stand by.

"Just go home, Harvey," Mr. Gilmore finally says. "Everybody just go home."

I stare at him speechlessly. He's going to end his party over something like this? Seriously?

I stand still. I don't know whether I should move. Do I have to clean up now? Or should I go, too?

"Um," I make my presence known.

"No, you stay," he says sternly, watching as one by one everyone goes home.

I start collecting the first glasses. Meanwhile, the bartender is also sent home.

"So that just now," I hear from the background and turn around. Mr. Gilmore is standing behind me. "Sorry. It's just ...," he looks around and sits down on an empty chair. "I like you. As my employee, as a person. And when I saw that creep throwing himself at you, I lost control."

He likes me? What?

So why has he been so dismissive of me these past few weeks?

He stands up again and looks at me. His gaze almost pierces me. "And when I imagined that he could touch you ... I didn't like that either."

What?! He's jealous?

He comes closer to me. His hand rests on my shoulder and suddenly moves up along my neck until it rests on my chin and finally on my lips.

Again, I'm frozen. Mr. Gilmore likes me? That ice-cold man?

He pulls me to him and suddenly our lips touch.

I hold my breath and feel what this kiss triggers in me. A desire that I would never have guessed was inside me. Of course I've seen him. Mr. Gilmore. Registered how handsome he is. How hot ... but I never dared imagine anything more with him. After all, he is my boss. This aloof, stern boss...

I feel my knees give out. He catches me. Holds me with his strong arms.

"Are you okay?" he asks, smiling at me.

"Yeah, it's just ... it's so unexpected," I say honestly.

"Unexpected? Haven't you noticed my glances the last few weeks? I tried to fight it, I withdrew. But I couldn't anymore." Again he reaches for my face and kisses me. Very gently, but then more and more impetuously and urgently.

I let myself go for it. I claw at his shirt and let him grab me to carry me to the sofa.

We make out. Wild and passionate and suddenly I can't get enough. From his lips, from his taste, from the sounds he makes.

"Oh God, I want you," I whisper, seeing the gleam in his eyes.

He grabs me again, opens my blouse swinging so that the buttons fly wildly through the area. He unclasps my bra and greedily starts kneading my breasts and touching them with his lips.

"You're so hot," he whispers in my ear as he now unbuttons his own shirt and slips it over his shoulders. I watch as his trained upper body comes to light and as his muscles tense, while he now carefully opens my skirt and pulls it over my hips. Quickly I also strip down the panties and lay naked in front of him.

He bites his lips with pleasure before kissing me again and sliding his hand through my cleft. I am wet. I notice that.

Without warning, he pushes two fingers deep inside me and starts moving them inside me.

"Oh God," I moan into his ear. Skillfully he brings me within a very short time just before a climax. I claw with my hands in his shoulder. Moan, gasp.

Then he suddenly stops. Startled, I look at him. He grins.

"I'm not going to let you come yet," he says and unbuckles his belt to pull down his pants. Automatically I look down at him and notice his hard, big cock.

Whew. I straighten up, reach for him, but he just pushes me back onto the soft cushion of the sofa.

Again he kisses me while his spanking now slides through my legs. God, he turns me on so much.

I put my hands on his hips, wanting him to finally penetrate me. Fucks me.

But he grabs my hands with his hand and holds them together over my head.

"Not yet," he whispers hotly in my ear as his lips move over my neck again, giving me violent goosebumps.

With his other hand he runs through my cleft again, touches my clit and teases it. Immediately I wince. "Oh fuck," I mumble and close my eyes.

And then the time has finally come. He puts his cock in and penetrates me with a violent push.

Sharply I suck in the air as I feel him inside me.

He starts to move around. Pushes himself in and out again and again. He quickens the pace.

Then he grabs me again and turns me around. With my belly I now lie on the sofa. At the hip he pulls me to him and penetrates me again.

Jesus. I never expected something like this to happen.

His thrusts become harder, his moans louder.

Then he puts a finger on my clit and rubs it. Shit. I stand again, just before a climax.

He continues. Rubs and fucks me.

And then it comes over me. I come. But he does not give me a breather. While I moan out my lust, he continues.

Fuck me. Sometimes slowly and with pleasure. Sometimes fast and hard.

He grabs me again. Turns me around. In his eyes I can see the lust. Again he presses his lips on my neck while he penetrates me with pleasure. Then he leans back. Goes down on his knees and puts my legs over his shoulders, while he does not take his eyes off me.

I tremble with pleasure and close my eyes again when I feel the next climax approaching. Oh God.

He thrusts more controlled now, puts his finger on my clit again and this little touch makes me explode again. Fuck.

Almost simultaneously, he also comes. I feel him jerk and pour into me. He has his eyes closed and holds my legs tightly. He takes one deep breath and blinks carefully.

A broad smile is on his face. "Oh wow," he gasps breathlessly. "I didn't expect that."

Carefully, he pulls out of me and drops down next to me on the sofa. Gently he caresses my naked body while he comes to rest again.

Speechless, I remain lying next to him. I didn't expect this either. Not even in my wildest dreams. And now? What will happen next?

"What's on your mind?" he asks me.

"I," I begin and want to shake my head. I want to tell him that I don't think anything. But that's not true. "What happens now?" I want to know.

"With us?"

"Yes."

"Well. So first of all, I'm going to grab you right now and carry you upstairs to the bedroom and eat you out one more time..."

"And after that?"

"I could use some sleep after that."

"No, how do we go on? Does it go on at all?" I ask hopefully.

He looks at me again. His look becomes more serious. "Well, I hope so," he replies and kisses me.

Reassured, I let myself fall into his arms. I hope so too ...

My club, my rules

"Vacation at last!" my best friend Anne exclaims, toasting me with her cocktail. Relaxed, she leans back on the deck chair and looks out over our turquoise-blue pool, behind which the hilly landscape of Mallorca stretches out. "It's hard to believe it really worked out with this house here."

"It's been a tough road," I merely agree with her, thinking about the drama of the last few weeks. We live in a beautiful AirBnB house in the north of Mallorca. Five bedrooms, a huge living room plus a gorgeous roof terrace and a spacious garden with pool. The two of us would never have been able to afford it, which is why we had to round up a few people. Six more, to be exact. We had a hard time choosing. Eight people for one week in a bunch. You have to be very selective. Neither of us have a large, common circle of friends. A few girlfriends here and there. Work colleagues or old fellow students from college.

"The mommies are already falling out," Anne said right at the beginning. "And the married ones, too." We wanted to go on a singles vacation. So that each can go without bad conscience also times to the Puppen celebrate and in the evening was not the time for telephone calls with the dearest one, but with beer and grill in the evening is spent.

"I think it's going to be good," Anne says, looking at the motley group that is gradually joining us at the pool and spreading out on the lounge chairs.

"So, what are we doing today?" wants to know Olivia, who has sat down at the edge of the pool to dip her bare feet in the cold water.

"Shopping. Best for the whole week," Anne suggests, waving an empty notepad around in her hand. "The nearest supermarket is just under 5km away. Half of us go there by car and buy everything. The other half will stay here."

I stay behind while Anne goes with the other half and packs the entire trunk of one of our rental cars.

When they are back, we stow all the supplies and prepare a wonderful dinner in the garden. We drink, make plans for the next days and splash in the pool.

"Here's to us!" exclaims Anne as we all sit in the pool with a cocktail and look up into the starry sky.

In the next few days we explore the island. Although we are in Mallorca, we have little interest in constantly drunk hanging out at Ballermann. We visit the different beaches, make excursions and go out for a fancy dinner. But one evening we also let ourselves be seduced to take a look at the tourist places. But I quickly find out that this is not for me at all. The pop music, the old, drunken men and the many Germans who completely misbehave.

"A friend told me about the many fancier beach clubs that are supposed to be here as well," suggests one of our number, and that definitely sounds more interesting. We pick something out and end up making a day trip out of it. We chill on the beach, drink cocktails and enjoy the, admittedly, overpriced food. In the evening, there is also a party there, to which we decide to go.

When I disappear to the toilet alone at some point and then get something to drink at the bar, I immediately notice the interested look of a man. Uncertainly, I return his gaze and realise that he is incredibly attractive. With my drink in my hand, I stop for a brief moment to give him a chance to approach me. Sure enough, he approaches me. His blue eyes sparkle as he faces me directly. I can smell his tangy perfume and feel my heart beating faster. When I'm out and about, it happens from time to time that I'm approached. But rarely is my counterpart so handsome.

"Hello," he says in an outrageously deep voice. "I'm Jorge. I own the club," he introduces himself directly.

"Hi," I reply quietly. "I'm Lilly." Uncertainly, I stop in front of him while he examines me with interest.

"Nice to meet you." He smiles when he gets back to my face. "Enjoying your evening?" he finally asks.

"Yes, it's ... quite nice here," I return, at which his smile widens.

"Just nice?"

"So ...", I say and look around. It's crowded and noisy. Over the course of the day, more and more people have rushed in. Especially since the party is in full swing. During the day it was still pleasantly empty, but by now I really long for our empty house. "It's already very crowded," I explain to him, while a woman pushes me aside to make her way to the bar.

"I see," he replies curtly, eyeing me one more time. "If you want, we can go somewhere else."

"Somewhere else?", I repeat. I can't leave the club after all. Not without telling my friends. And especially not with a complete stranger.

"I think ...", I begin and am about to say no, but he cuts me off.

"To the VIP area," he explains quickly, pointing to a staircase leading up.

"Oh," it escapes me and I follow his gaze. I realise that the staircase is cordoned off with a black velvet ribbon and that only selected guests seem to be able to pass through there. My curiosity is aroused. I wonder what's hiding up there? "Okay," I finally say and see him grin.

I follow him and when we are standing in front of the security man at the stairs, he loosens the barrier tape without difficulty so that we can get through. Mh. I wonder who he is?

We go up and find ourselves on a roof terrace, which is pleasantly empty. From here you have a great view of the open sea. There are comfortable lounge chairs everywhere and on a small dance floor there are a few people dancing to Spanish music.

We move toward the table, which is directly on the glass railing and thus offers the best view of the beach. The table is fully occupied, but when they see who is approaching them, the three men stand up and reverently make room for Jorge.

"Here you go," they murmur, pointing to the empty seats.

"Thank you," I reply, confused, and just wondering one more time who my companion is. Hopefully not a mafia boss or the like.

"I own the place," he tells me, because he must have noticed my hesitation.

"Ah," I say, and am relieved. That explains a lot, of course.

"And this is my regular table." He leans way back into the soft cushion, then waves one of the waiters over. "What would you like to drink?"

"Moscow Mule," I reply immediately, to which Jorge nods as well. "Make it two."

He leans forward and looks at me. "What are you doing here on the island, Lilly?" he asks, and I'm flattered that he remembered my name. And also that he approached me, of all people, and brought me upstairs with him.

"I'm on vacation with a couple of girlfriends," I explain, suddenly feeling very small. Sitting across from me is such an attractive and successful man, and I'm just ... me.

"How nice. Are they here, too?" he wants to know.

"Yeah, they're down at the club somewhere."

Knowingly, he nods. "Next time you come here, you can all come right up," he offers generously. "It's not quite so ... crowded here," he teases me, alluding to my comment just now.

I feel caught. "Thank you," I murmur and immediately reach for the drink that the waiter now brings us. I hurriedly pull on the straw and drink almost half the glass. I really need to loosen up.

We talk. About our vacation, about our house and the activities we have already done here and will still do.

Jorge is nice. The conversation is nice. And yet somehow I feel like I'm at a job interview. As if I had to prove myself. I don't know why.

After a few hours, my cell phone rings and I realise how late it already is. "My girlfriends are looking for me," I explain as I get up.
He waves an employee over and points at me. "Show him your girlfriends. He'll look for them and bring them up."

Surprised, I look at him. What a nice offer!

I dig out a picture and immediately he sets off to look for them.

Then we continue our conversation. So far he has made no effort to come closer to me, but now he slides a little from his chair in my direction.

"I really like you, Lillly," he says, looking deep into my eyes.

I'm getting dizzy. Is this really happening right now?

"There you are!" we are suddenly interrupted and I hear the drunken voices of my friends. When I turn around, they're all standing behind me, looking around with wide eyes. Then, one by one, each of their gazes falls on Jorge. It's written all over their faces that they immediately want to know how I got to know him.

"Sit down," Jorge offers, vacating his seat. "I'll get you something to drink."

He gets up and as soon as he's out of earshot, the girls start pestering me with questions. But I don't have any answers myself. "I don't know what he wants from me. We were just talking. And then he came for you. Nothing has happened yet."

"Well, he certainly doesn't lack for attractive women here," she remarks after taking another thorough look around. I, too, now let my gaze wander over the roof terrace. All the tables are occupied. The proportion of women actually predominates. He had no reason to lure more women upstairs to make it more attractive to the other guests. That was it, too, before my girlfriends were led here.

"Maybe he's just really nice," Olivia suggests, to which everyone eyes her suspiciously.

"As if," Anne interjects again. "He's probably up to something."

"Maybe he just thinks I'm very nice?", I speak up now.

"If he wanted to sleep with you, all he had to do was talk to you down on the dance floor and not lead you and your entire following up here," Anne says. For a moment, I'm offended. But she is right. Jorge is not only incredibly attractive, but also very charming. He didn't have to put on such a show to get me into bed.

"For the ladies," he interrupts our conversation and stands in front of us with a silver tray containing a chilled bottle of champagne as well as glasses.

One after the other, Jorge hands us each a glass and fills it with the sparkling liquid. We all exchange another uncertain glance, but then join him in a toast. I watch Anne take a tiny sip and then place her glass on the table. She is unsettled. Something strange is going on here, and I have this thought, too. But then I look at Jorge, who has drained his glass in one go. He was drinking from the same bottle. He wouldn't do that if he had mixed something into our drink. Besides, he opened the bottle here at the table. How is that supposed to work?

I decide that I will not let myself be unsettled. Maybe he's only being so nice to me because he actually likes me. And because he noticed that I wanted to leave when the girls contacted me, he let himself be led upstairs so that I would stay.

I drink the last bit from my glass and now turn back to Jorge, who is sitting contentedly in his armchair, gazing at the calming sea.

"Shall we dance?", I ask him boldly, to which he smiles and his eyes sparkle at me again.

"I'd love to," he replies and immediately stands up. He holds out his hand to me and the two of us move toward the small dance floor at the edge of the roof terrace.

I feel the looks of the others at my back, but at the same time I notice that they relax again. No one wants to do us any harm here. I'm sure of that.

We dance. First very loosely, then tightly embrace and finally we come closer. His lips press on mine, while his hands enclose my body.

I feel this crackling between us. The sexual attraction is almost tangible.

"Let's go somewhere else," he says firmly, and I don't dare contradict him. Taking my hand, he leads me off the dance floor and brings me back downstairs. There we go through a small side entrance into another part of the club. It almost seems like a small apartment.

"This is where I like to retreat to when I need some quiet time."

I remain silent and notice the peace that reigns here. No booming bass, no screeching when the next champagne bottle is opened. Nothing. One hears absolutely nothing.

He switches on the light and leads me into a spacious living room. This small apartment, which he uses as a retreat, is larger than the apartment I live in.

I look around uncertainly and finally take a seat on the deep sofa while he stands in the open kitchen and opens the refrigerator.

"What would you like to drink?" he asks me.

I shrug my shoulders. "What's wrong?"

"Anything you want."

"Moscow Mule it is."

I hear him open a bottle with a crown cap, fill ice cubes into a cup and cut something. A little later, he stands in front of me with a cool cup and holds the drink out to me.

"Here you go," he says, toasting me with his mug before dropping down next to me on the soft sofa.

Waiting, I remain seated next to him. I am so unsure. Why did he bring me here? Why is he making me a drink first, when it's all about us having sex right away anyway?

He puts his hand on my knee and gently strokes my bare skin as his intense gaze pierces me. "What are you thinking about?" he asks me.

Immediately, I shake my head. "Oh, nothing." I look at him, watching as he slowly leans over me, takes my cup and puts it on the plate, and then starts kissing me.

I quickly lie wide-legged under him. He with his body between my legs. I feel how he rubs himself urgently against me and his cock becomes harder and harder. Slowly he takes me off and soon I'm sitting in front of him with only a slip.

"Let's go to the bedroom," he finally says, standing up and reaching for my hand. As he leads me into the next dark room, he unbuttons his shirt and undoes his belt.

Hardly has he turned on the light, he pushes me already belly-down on the big bed and begins to litter my back with kisses. Mhh ...

56

Again he grabs me and turns me around. I lie under him again and look into his eyes, which he keeps half closed.

All of a sudden, I hear a noise. A door is being opened. "What's that?" I ask, startled, but he doesn't move.

"That will probably just be my business partner. He uses the apartment, too."

I stare wide-eyed at the open bedroom door. He can't see us here, can he? I pause, hearing several voices. Several men's voices.

"And they're just coming into the apartment here now?", I ask nervously.

He shrugs his shoulders. "You got a problem with that?" He starts kissing my neck and his hand moves between my legs. Jesus. He immediately finds the right spot, which is why I close my eyes and start moaning. "No," I whisper softly. "It's no problem." As long as he keeps doing what he's doing right now, why would that be a problem for me?

Slowly he pushes my panties off my hips and starts fingering me with his skillful hands. I feel myself getting wetter and hornier. I want to feel him. Right now.

I push myself towards his crotch, reach out to him so that I can at least touch him. But he holds me tight. He grabs my hands with one hand and holds them over my head. Then he looks at me again. Intensively and decisively. I can't help it and give in. I am like putty in his hands. He can do anything he wants with me.

Suddenly the voices get louder. "Don't you want to close the door?" I ask cautiously.

"Nah, why? It's exciting when they can hear us." At that, he grins and kisses me again.

That's right ... it's exciting. So I block out the voices and close my eyes again.

He grabs me again, turns me around and again I lie on my stomach. He puts my arms in front of me and then grabs me by the waist to pull me up. I hear the rustling of fabric. He takes off his underpants. I want to turn around. Get a glimpse of his hard cock, but he pushes me down by the shoulder. God, why does his dominance make me so hot?

I wince as I feel him slide his hard spanking through my wet cleft. In a moment it's time. In a moment I can feel him.

And then it finally happens. With one hard thrust he penetrates me completely.

I groan out loud so that he understands how much I like what he is doing with me.

His grip strengthens as he takes me harder and faster.

My hands claw into the sheet as I moan and gasp exuberantly.

God, does that feel good.

He, too, becomes louder. Our skin claps against each other in a clearly audible way, but by now I have

58

completely blocked out the fact that we are not alone. The men can hear us. They must hear us, because no one here tries to be quiet anymore.

But then it's over all at once. A few more times Jorge pushes hard into me before he comes.

Somewhat disappointed, I let myself fall onto the bed. Was that it already?

I turn around and see him carefully getting up from the bed and reaching for a handkerchief. He grins at me. "That was awesome," he says and then marches naked into the adjoining bathroom.

I remain confused and look at him irritated when he comes back into the room freshly showered and wrapped in a towel.

"I hope you can still?" he asks me as he starts to get dressed again.

Hesitantly, I shake my head. "I thought you were done," I say, confused, and reach for my clothes as well.

"I am, but actually ... that was just foreplay," he explains to me, pointing to the men in the next room. "I'm actually more into watching the woman I think is hot get fucked by my co-workers."

I open my mouth in shock. What?! Suddenly two men appear in the bedroom. In the bedroom where I am still lying naked on the bed. I try to cover myself, but then look into their enthusiastic faces in turn, until I finally arrive at Jorge, who is still looking down at me horny.

"Or is that too much for you?"

Once again, I take a closer look at the two of them. They are tall and athletic, have dark hair and masculine faces. They are exactly my type, but I can't do that so easily ... Have sex with three men in one evening?

On the other hand ... what's stopping me?

"You can say no, of course. But then the evening would be over at this point."

I think about it. I waver back and forth between "no, you can't do that" and "when will I ever get this opportunity?" until I finally nod hesitantly. "All right."

Jorge smiles. "I knew it. I knew right from the start that you'd be into it."

He buttons up his shirt and finally takes a seat on an armchair in the corner of the room. With wide eyes I follow how the two unknown men undress and their perfectly trained bodies are revealed under the dark clothes. Whew ...

The first one comes to me on the bed and starts kissing me. I let myself go for it, touch his strong arms, his muscular back and finally his hard bump. The second now also comes to us in bed, kisses me before he then disappears between my legs and starts to rub me with his fingers.

God ... I'm so horny and about to explode.

I am grabbed and turned around. Again I lie on the bed and feel hands on my hips, I notice how I literally run out and how again a tail slides through my wet column.

"Oh God," I moan out loud as I feel the second cock of the evening inside me. All this is so horny. The looks of Jorge on me, the two unknown men next to me.

I hear more voices and out of the corner of my eye I see more men enter the room. I want to say something. Want to protest, but at the same moment a tail is shoved into my mouth.

What do I want to say? Jorge would not accept that I say no anyway and just the idea that I have to submit to his wishes makes me even hornier.

So I try to turn off my head and just enjoy. I enjoy how the big cock just bores into my neck. How a second just takes me hard from behind. And even the thumb that carefully makes its way into my ass, I enjoy. For a long time I had the dream of how it would be to be fucked by two men in the ass and pussy at the same time and I think that this dream could come true today.

I see the next man getting ready. How he puts his clothes on a chair and comes to me on the bed. The thrusts become harder and I hear how the unknown man comes behind me. Right after that I taste something bitter in my mouth and see how the one in front of me slowly pulls out his twitching cock and lets me lick it clean. Oh man. I never thought I would do something like this, but it's incredibly horny.

The two are immediately exchanged and the next are the turn. One on my hip, the other grabs my head. Again two big spanks drill into me and start to fuck me. Another finger is drilled into my butt, stretching and widening me. Makes me ready for what is about to come.

Suddenly Jorge appears next to me. In his eyes I recognise the horniness. He grins and his pants are already all bulging. "You're so hot," he whispers and watches very closely as I take the big cock in my throat.

Again I am grabbed. The beating leaves my mouth and suddenly I sit astride the man below me. He grabs me by the waist and lifts me up on his hard cock. I groan as I feel him so deep inside me and then I am pushed forward onto his chest.

The men fall silent and no one moves. Until they have decided among themselves who is next. I feel how the bed shakes and someone kneels behind me. Again the finger in my ass, which is immediately exchanged with a cock. The man under me holds me with both arms while the man behind me now slowly penetrates me.

"Oh God," I groan as I notice the second cock disappearing piece by piece in my ass. A mixture of horniness and pain spreads through me, but I grit my teeth until he is finally completely inside me. I hear Jorge cheering them on and then they start to move slowly.

I squint my eyes and slowly get used to this unfamiliar, but mega-awesome feeling. It feels incredible. The two become faster. The feeling inside me stronger. I moan and gasp louder and louder. The two men also get in on it. The first one comes and immediately the second one follows. I am held again, the men detach themselves from me and make room for the next.

And so it goes on. No idea how many men Jorge has called to his small apartment, but each one I take in me and make him come. I myself have been made to come countless times. With the tongue, with the fingers or just with the tail.

I am tired and exhausted, but at the same time I never want this to end.

I just take another load of cum in my mouth when Jorge announces that I have had enough now.

Dazed, I carefully climb up from the bed and try to keep myself on my feet. My knees hurt, my back aches. I can barely hold myself upright.

Beaming, Jorge looks at me. "Just look at you. You really enjoyed it, didn't you?"

I nod and see him open his pants. His bulging cock falls out. I feel a pressure on my shoulder and fall back onto the bed. He moves me into position. My head on the sheet, my butt stretched up. Then he penetrates me. Again he fucks me. This time harder and more continuous than the first time. When he comes, he moans loudly and shouts out how horny he found this night.

When he's done, he turns me to him. "Come back to my club anytime and I'll give you another night like this."

After that, he gets dressed and leaves me alone in the room. On wobbly legs I go into the bathroom and let the hot water run over my body. Afterwards I tie a bathrobe around me and come into the living room. The men have disappeared. Jorge too.

He left money for the cab and his cell phone number.

I have another drink from the fridge, get dressed and then call a cab. But I will be back. For sure.

At the party in front of everyone

Anxiously, I take a look inside the mailbox and can already see the many white envelopes through the slot. Nervously, I put the key in the hole and open the door. I take out the letters addressed to me and already know what's inside: Final reminder. In 5-fold. Damn!

I lost my job a few weeks ago and haven't found anything new yet. The bills are piling up and slowly I just don't know what to do.

"More reminders?" my roommate Mel asks me, looking anxiously at the stack of letters in my hand.

Hesitantly, I nod. "I only have a week left to pay them. And my bank account is empty. Not to mention my wallet. What am I going to do?"

Mel is silent and just looks at me. "So..." she starts, but I know exactly what she's getting at. She's been working part-time as an escort for a while now and regularly raves to me about how great she thinks it is and that I could give it a try. But so far everything in me has resisted.

"I don't know," I start, and I still can't imagine how something like that is supposed to happen.

She pauses again and takes a look at her hands. Then she starts to grin. "Tonight is such an event, it's being held privately at a customer's home. I've never been there myself and never met him, but my colleague Kim has. I guess he does it quite often. Almost every month and every time she really looks forward to it, because this one evening not only brings her a lot of money, but she also has a lot of fun. He always invites a bunch of people: Business partners, friends and acquaintances and also a few escorts. I asked her if I could come along this time and if you want, I'm sure I can sneak you in. Then you can take a closer look at it all."

"And then?", I ask, confused.

"Then you're either making a pile of money, too, or at worst, you've had an exciting evening."

"Mh," I say, unable to imagine anything under her description. "And who's that?"

Mel shrugs her shoulders. "All I know is that she likes to meet with the client. He's attractive and generous. I'm honestly always a little jealous when he gets back to her. But maybe I'll find one there, too."

With that, she turns away from me and disappears into her room to get ready for the evening. I stay behind in the kitchen, with the threatening reminders in my hand.

Mh. Once again I think, but what do I have to lose? As she said, either I can pay my debts after this evening or I had an insight into such a party. Nobody will force me to do something I don't want to do.

So I agree and a little later I'm standing together with Mel in front of her closet and together we pick out something for me to wear.

Nervously, I tug at the short dress that Mel has lent me for this evening. It just about covers my buttocks, but accentuates my long legs quite well.

66

"Not so fast," I say as I trot along a little awkwardly on my high heels behind Mel and Kim.

"Now hurry up," Kim prompts me, who is now standing right in front of her client's large estate. "It already started half an hour ago. Mark hates tardiness."

"It's not my fault the cab was late," I whine.

"But you can very well help it if we're even later now."

She stands in front of the imposing gate and presses the bell. "This is Kim. Accompanied by two friends," I hear her say into the intercom, whereupon a loud buzz sounds and the gate is opened.

The three of us quickly scurry through it and walk up the long driveway to the front door.

"Oh man," I mutter as we stand in front of the entrance, where numerous expensive cars have already gathered. As if by magic, the next door also opens and I feel as if I've fallen through some process and now find myself in a completely different world.

"Wow," I say, impressed, as I stand in this fabulously decorated house and see people in colourful costumes standing around celebrating everywhere.

"Mark probably should have let me know the theme," Kim says, staring down at her black dress.

"No problem. There seems to be a costume room," Mel says, pointing to a room in front of which a long line has formed. One by one, the waiting people disappear and come out in costume.

"Luckily," she says and joins the queue as well. Mel and I follow her, and while we wait, I have a chance to look around more. It's ... I don't even know what to compare this to. I've never experienced anything like this before.

The people are shrill, it's loud, and yet everything seems so ... orderly. It's almost as if they're all waiting for a starting signal so that things can finally get underway.

"There you are," Kim is greeted by a handsome man who will surely be Mark. He gives her a peck on the cheek left and right and then looks in my direction. "And these are your girlfriends?" he asks, emphasising the last word quite strangely.

"Yeah, right," Kim quickly replies, grinning in our direction.

"How nice. Then we'll certainly have the pleasure later," he says, giving me a particularly long look before disappearing into the crowd again.

"What does that mean?" I immediately ask.

"He thinks you're an escort," Mel explains to me excitedly.

"What?!", I ask in shock, remembering at the same moment why I am actually here and falling silent again.

"Next!" the woman in the "costume box" calls, looking at us expectantly.

"Mm," she mutters, looking at us one at a time. "Ah, got it." While she hands out princess dresses to Mel and Kim, I fittingly get an Alice in Wonderland costume.

"It's like she guessed how I was feeling right now," I say as I look at myself in the mirror with the other two.

"Well then. I'm going for a spin," Kim says to us, and before we can say anything back, she's already gone.

"I thought we were staying together," I say, dumbfounded, and give Mel a look, who is also already looking around impatiently.

"She's saving up for a car and probably wants to speed it up," she merely explains to me, suddenly extending her hand in a wave. "I'll be right back," she calls to me and hurries toward someone I don't know. All of a sudden I'm standing there all alone.

And now?

I look around in search of help. But what do I expect? That I will suddenly meet someone familiar here? An old friend from school? A former colleague?

I hope not.

So I do what I always do when I'm left alone for a moment when I go out: I go to the bar.

Confidently, I push past the people and stand at the bar. I watch the people ahead of me to decide what I want to drink and decide to take the same as the woman in front of me.

"Here you go," the bartender says, handing me a dark red cocktail.

Curiously, I sip on the golden metal straw and am relieved to find that the drink tastes pretty good. Strong, but there's enough sugar and juice in it that even I can drink it. I then take my first spin and look around.

People are standing everywhere who are a bit older than me and already seem well on their way to drunk. They are talking animatedly, dancing to the loud music, but at the same time still seem as if they are waiting for something. Something exciting. Again and again they interrupt their conversation, cast a tense glance at the clock before they continue talking.

Like on New Year's Eve or before a birthday that's being celebrated.

"What are they all waiting for so eagerly?", I ask a woman who is about my age and also standing around alone.

"Well, for the show," she explains to me with a smile.

"What kind of show?", I want to know.

She wears a red velvet cape that covers her body. She briefly lifts it so that I can see the provocative underwear underneath. "Well, judging by this show and your outfit, I guess you're part of it too."

Irritated, I look at her.

"Oh, you're not one of the escorts? Sorry. I just thought, because the normal party guests are usually always a little older than me." With the words, she turns around and disappears into the crowd again.

What does she mean by that? What show?

Astonished, I continue walking and am suddenly touched by someone on the shoulder. Almost relieved, I turn around. After all, that can only be Mel, whom I can now finally confront.

But it's not Mel. It's Mark.

"At last we meet again," he greets me and hands me a glass of champagne. "Go ahead and drink it. You still seem very tense."

Uncertainly, I take the glass from his hand and sip from it.

"When Kim asked if she could bring some girlfriends, I wasn't very excited. I host these types of parties on a regular basis and like to have control over my guests and just the girls I invite. But when she showed up with you, I was really into it. Kim has been in the business for a long time. She's hot, no question, but also very hard-nosed. You, on the other hand, are ..." he confidently runs his hand over my arm, making me wince right away. "You still seem very ... new to the business. Almost innocent. I like that."

I take a deep breath. I'm new to the business. I haven't even started yet, so to speak. And I'm not even sure if this is the right thing for me. "Um," I say, pained, and look at him, his steel-blue eyes sternly scrutinising me. I can't tell him now that I just wanted to drop in here. This doesn't look like a party that an outsider can just drop in on. I'm sure the rest of the people here are paying a lot of money and in the end he wants me to pay the same amount as well if I'm not one of the girls putting on the show. Whatever that show is supposed to be.

I force myself to smile, whereupon Mark grins as well.

"Anyway, glad you're here. I'm looking forward to seeing you in a bit." He turns away again, leaving me alone.

I notice how my hands are suddenly all wet. Sweat forms on my forehead and I first have to get my bearings again. Where has Mel taken me?

I finish the glass of champagne in one go, set it down on some table, and then go in search of her.

Fortunately, I can find her quite quickly. She is currently with a man to whom she always makes beautiful eyes.

"Can I talk to you for a minute?", I whisper to her.

Horrified, she looks at me. "Can't it wait?" she mumbles as she gives the man next to her an apologetic look.

"No, it can't," I reply in a firm voice.

"All right." She whispers to the man that she'll be right back and lets me lead her to a quiet corner. "What's so important? That was Henry Parker over there. A real big shot in the art scene. He could really get me ahead career-wise."

"What kind of party is this?", I now ask her seriously.

72

She shrugs. "You know. Well-heeled people drink champagne together, dance, and eventually have fun together."

"So what?"

"What? You know how it is."

"No, I don't know that."

"Oh, come on, Kate. Don't tell me you don't know what this is."

I shake my head. I have no idea at all. "The people here are all swingers. Usually at 12 o'clock all the clothes come off, or like today, costumes, and then certain rooms open up and everyone...does it with each other."

I open my mouth. I really didn't expect this. I thought she was taking me to an ordinary party, where I might make a contact or two with a potential client. With a very wealthy client. "And what kind of show is that?", I now want to know.

Now she looks at me, confused. "Show?"

"There was this woman. Hardly older than me. She was wearing a Little Red Riding Hood costume and some pretty provocative lingerie underneath. She said something about a show she was in and she thought I was in it, too."

"Mh ... well. Mark pays each of us a lot of money. He'll expect something for that. Maybe there'll be a little interlude to heat things up."

"A little interlude?"

"Now don't act so naive, Kate. Either among ourselves, or with a callboy, or even with one of the guests. That's for starters. Before it really gets going."

I become quite pale. That I would possibly have sex here with a man who is a stranger to me is one thing. But that I will also have it in front of all the people is quite another.

Mel puts a hand on my shoulder. "You're not being forced to do anything. If you feel uncomfortable, you can leave at any time. And you don't have to do anything you don't want to, either."

"Mh," I say, thinking again about the reminders that are lying at home. That's no way to pay them.

"You can maybe just watch for now and who knows ... maybe you'll feel like joining in after all. So ... all I can tell you is that the feeling of being in the middle and being watched by everyone while you give in to your lust ... it's just incredible." Now she starts to smile. "But I guess you'll have to find out for yourself."

All of a sudden a gong sounds and people start moving eagerly.

"Here we go!" they murmur excitedly and rush toward the stairs.

"What happens now?", I ask Mel, although I already know the answer.

She grabs my hand and a little later we also meet Kim, who nods at us.

"Here we go!" she repeats the words of the others and drags us behind her.

Without being able to say anything, I follow her.

We arrive in a room big enough for all the other guests. And us.

In the middle is a small pedestal. A podium that is laid out with several mattresses, padded benches and other reclining options. I feel quite different when I look around and see the guests looking up expectantly.

Then Mark appears. He confidently steps onto the small platform and looks down at his friends and acquaintances from above. He smiles. "Good evening," he greets us and seems amused. He is wearing a colourful royal costume, of which only the crown and red trousers remain. His steeled upper body is exposed.

"I'm glad to see that there are so many of us again this time," and now he looks in our direction. "And I'm glad that a few new faces have joined us today as well."

My heart is beating like crazy. Surely he's not about to ask me to sit on this pedestal?

"Kim? Where are you?" he asks, and I feel Kim push past me and scurry upstairs. As she stands next to Mark, she bows playfully. The crowd cheers her on.

"What do we want to start with today?" he asks Kim, who merely looks at him innocently. "Okay. Let's ask the audience instead. What do you want Kim to start with today? What do you want her to do for a living today?" he shouts.

Kim just grins and waits for the answers. When someone shouts something, she holds her hand to her ear to show that she didn't understand.

"What was that?" she murmurs softly.

"Fuck you with a dildo!" it sounds louder in response.

She grins again and rummages around in a box that is also on the stage. She pulls out a purple dildo and holds it up. "With this?" she asks, and again everyone cheers.

I watch, slightly shocked, as she lifts her skirt and quickly pulls her panties off her hips. Then she lies down on one of the benches and spreads her legs. You can see everything. She then pushes the dildo first into her mouth to moisten it and then into her pussy.

I am petrified. Is this really happening right now?

Kim starts fucking herself with the dildo while people watch and crowd closer to the platform.

Mark continues talking and brings another young woman over. It is the one I met earlier. She is now standing next to him and again Mark asks what she should do.

"I want to fuck her!" someone shouts, stretching his arm upwards.

"All right, then come here," Mark replies, and a little later a middle-aged man stands in front of the young woman and pulls down his pants. Without resistance, she lies down on one of the mattresses and spreads her legs. Just as he penetrates her, someone taps my shoulder.

"Mark is waiting for you," a young man tells me, looking me straight in the face.

"Me?" I ask, confused, pointing at myself.

"Yes." He turns around and expects me to follow him. But I can't move. What does that mean, he is expecting me?

"Go on," Mel urges me, and I trot after the man.

When I stop in front of the pedestal, he goes again and leaves me alone. I have no clue what to do now. When I look up, Mark is no longer there.

"Ah, there you are," he greets me, suddenly standing in front of me.

"Yes...", I reply uncertainly.

"Are you ready?"

"For what?"

Now he looks confused. "You're not an escort are you?"

I hesitate with my answer and then carefully shake my head.

"Then what are you doing here?" He almost seems a little angry.

"Well, actually ...", I start, but I don't know how to finish the sentence and therefore decide to be completely honest. "Well, actually, I was hoping that maybe I could make a little money here. My roommate is an escort and she took me with her. However, I didn't know what exactly to expect here."

"I see ... well, this isn't the right place to just take a look," he looks around at his coworker. Surely he's going to kick me out now. "You'd better go back now." His intense gaze almost pierces me.

"But ...", I say and again I don't know what to say. On the one hand, I want to go home. Want to leave all this behind. On the other hand, I'm curious. I want to know what happens next. I want to know what else is going to happen on this pedestal and, above all, I want to know what it's like when the rest of them drop their inhibitions, too. And besides ... besides, there are the reminders waiting for me at home. I can't go. Impossible! "What would I have to do?", I therefore ask.

Interested, Mark looks at me. "Are you serious?"

"Yes."

"Well, what we tell you. You can always say no, of course, but," now he leans down to me. "The more you do, the more money you get in the end." He winks at me.

Something inside me is bubbling. It's the excitement. And at the same time, the excitement I feel at his words. The more you do, the more money you get in the end. Words that used to leave me cold and now they suddenly trigger something in me. The idea turns me on. Very much so.

"Okay," I say again. "I'm in."

His smile widens. "How nice. I'm glad." He takes my hand and we walk back to the podium where we are not the only ones. Still, I feel the stares on me as I stand at the top and Mark addresses his word to his guests.

"We have a new addition here today. This is Lilly. This is her first time here."

I am applauded. People are cheering, calling my name. I feel great. Still, my heart is pounding. What's next?

Mark beams at me. "So ... what should we do with her?" he asks.

"I want to fuck her!" shouts the first one. I keep a lookout for the man. A guy in his early 50s with a beer belly and a balding forehead. Jesus. What am I doing here?

I try to smile and not let anything show. Suddenly I feel Mark's arm on my shoulder.

"Well," he begins. "I think I'll take the privilege of hosting for today and go first. Initiate our new addition into our ranks, so to speak. What do you think?"

I exhale in relief. Everything I've imagined in the last few minutes has taken place with Mark. In fact, I was even hoping he'd be the one to fuck me. Not that guy there.

Again the people cheer. "Yes! We want to see her take your huge cock in her mouth!"

Expectantly I look at Mark, who then just grins and opens his pants. To see, I actually get a huge beating and swallow hard. How should it fit in my mouth? Let alone in any other orifices?

But again I try to turn off my head. It will work out somehow. I get on my knees, embrace his cock with my hand, which then gets a little harder.

I look up and see him smile at me and then put his hands on my head, pointing me in the right direction. His glans touches my lips, I moisten it with my tongue and slowly let him slide into my mouth. Again the crowd cheers.

I put my head wide in my neck and let Mark fuck me deeper and deeper in my throat, because for some reason it makes me horny. To kneel here in front of the others and satisfy him. Or rather, *having* to satisfy him. I really enjoy it.

But then he stops and pulls me back up by my arm. "That wasn't bad for a start." He points down at me. "Take your clothes off."

I don't hesitate for a second and get rid of my clothes. I am so horny for him that I would do anything he would tell me at that moment.

"Lean over this," he says, pointing to a small velvet bench. I prop myself up with my upper body. My knees are on the floor. Is he going to fuck me now?

No, instead I feel a pain on my butt. He hits me with the flat of his hand. I close my eyes, start to groan, and then bite my lips. Jesus. Then he stops. His fingers run through my crack, making me wince. He laughs. "If you could feel how wet she is," he announces, amused, and gives me another slap, making me groan again. Why does this turn me on so much?

"Mm," he says, taking his hand away again. "Which one of you wants to feel how wet she is?"

My heart beats faster. What is happening now? I try to take a look over my shoulder and see numerous people raising their hands.

"Sally!" he calls out. "You may come to me."

I hear footsteps and a little later I see the flowing fabric of a long skirt behind me. The woman goes down on her knees and then I notice her fingers on my crotch and how she drives once through my cleft. "Oha. She's really wet," she says enthusiastically and then also pushes a finger deep into my pussy. Again I moan.

"Hey, not so fast!", Mark stops her. "But while you're at it ... go ahead."

Another finger slides inside me and she starts fucking me with it. Meanwhile, my fingers claw at the bench. In the meantime I have blanked out everything around me. I just want to be fucked.

"Okay, that's enough," I hear Mark say, and the woman pulls away. "My turn now."

My heart does a little hop. Is he finally fucking me now?

Again I feel his hand between my legs and then finally something else. Something bigger. His cock. He lets it slide up and down once. Moistens it with my juice and then ... then he finally pushes it into me.

I'm rearing up. Shit, he's big. He grabs my waist, holds me tight and then starts to fuck me. With hard, powerful thrusts. Again I squeeze my eyes shut, moan and gasp. God, this feels so good. He continues, fucking me harder and faster. Now I hear him, too. He sighs, snorts loudly and speeds up once more. Violently my hips are pressed against the bench, but I do not care. He should just keep going.

And then he comes. Loud and violently twitching. I feel how he pours into me. How he clutches my hip and how his climax slowly subsides. He lets go of me and straightens up. It takes me a moment. My knees ache, my legs shake. That was intense.

Mark reaches out for me and slowly I stand up again. I look at the people below me, who look at me lustfully. Some kiss each other, others touch each other. There are even a few who fuck each other here. In pairs, in threes or even in fours.

"And now?", I ask, looking at the exhausted Mark.

"Go down and enjoy yourself," he tells me, then gets off the pedestal.

Once again I look around. Kim has disappeared. There is no trace of Mel either when I find myself in the middle of the crowd.

"Hey," a couple addresses me and smiles at me. They are half naked and holding hands. "Would you like to come with us?" they ask me, pointing to one of the rooms in the back.

"Um," I say, finally shaking my head. She looked like my old maths teacher, and besides, I want to look around a bit myself first.

I continue on my way and watch people doing it with each other without restraint. I get curious, take a look in every room and am asked almost every time if I want to join in. But so far nothing has appealed to me.

Until I suddenly find myself in a room that arouses my curiosity even more than the rest.

A young woman is in the centre. She is tied to a gynaecological chair and her eyes are blindfolded. Around her are several men and women. They have sex toys in their hands and there is a cube in the middle.

"My turn!" shouts one woman as her number appears on the cube. She walks up to the young woman in the middle and starts working her over with a large dildo. The young woman moans and cries out. I see her pelvis twitch and her hands bury themselves in her bonds. And then I feel something else. And that is how the sight of the woman turns me on.

"Do you want to play?" one of the men asks me, holding out his dice and the toy in his hand. "I was going on anyway."

But I shake my head. I want to participate, but not as a player. I want to be the woman in the middle. "I can relieve her," I say and point to the woman, who looks exhausted.

"Oh, good. She already asked a few rounds ago, but no one came yet," he explains to me with a grin. Just the idea that I have to stay there until a replacement comes makes me even hornier. What's wrong with me?

The woman's blindfold is removed and her restraints loosened. Carefully she stands up and smiles at me when she sees that I will now take her place. "Have fun," she whispers to me and ties my eyes herself.

I am led to the chair. My hands and feet are tied. Then it starts. The dice fall and I notice someone walking towards me. I feel a vibration. A violent vibration on my clit. A vibration so violent that I can no longer pull myself together and come. Within a few seconds. I moan and gasp. "Stop!", I shout, trying to escape the strong stimulus that still touches my clit, but the person does not let go of me. Instead, she laughs.

"I noticed that you came. But it was too fast for me," says a woman and raises the step.

My entire body trembles. My butt tenses, my pelvis pushes up and then I come again. And one more time. Beads of sweat form on my forehead. I feel hot and exhausted. Then she finally lets go of me and it goes on.

Oh God, this is somehow not how I imagined it.

It's the next person's turn. I wince as something cold touches my clit. "Nice and sensitive," a man murmurs and runs something slick through my cleft.

Relieved, I groan when it is just a dildo that he now pushes into me and fucks me with it. But the relief does not last long, as his movements become stronger and harder. Again I am about to come, but he does not let me. Instead, he laughs wickedly.

It goes on. Another toy comes into play. It's something small and smooth that slides effortlessly into my pussy. No challenge at all. But then it's pulled back out and rests against my ass instead. Oh. I wince briefly as the little something gets stuck inside me and hear the person leave again. "I'll put out for a minute, but leave the plug in."

It goes on. Again I'm fucked, then worked with a vibrator and things put in me. It is horny, but at the same time exhausting and so slowly I also long for a relief.

After just under an hour, I'm at the end and I hear a young woman step up next to me and whisper to me whether she should relieve me.

"Yes, please," I say and feel my blindfold being removed. It is Kim who smiles at me.

"Are you having fun?" she asks, undoing my bonds.

"Oh yes," I answer honestly, even though all I'm currently craving is a shower and a bathrobe.

"Fine." She helps me off the chair and has to support me as I step onto the floor with wobbly legs.

"Before you go, check in with Mark so he can give you your money," she adds before climbing into the chair herself.

I seek out the nearest restroom, take a hot shower, and tap around the house barefoot and clad only in a towel. I have no idea where my costume is. My clothes should still be in the locker room, where I now go.

"Ah, there you are again," I hear a deep voice say. It's Mark. "Are you having a good time?" he asks me.

I start to smile. "Yes."

"I thought so." He leads me into a small side room and pulls out an envelope from the safe. "This is for you."

I accept the thick envelope and know that it must contain an extremely large amount of money. Even if there were only 5 euro bills inside, which I don't think there would be.

"Why don't you come back next month," he says as he closes the safe again.

"I will," I reply curtly and stow the money in my pocket.

I quickly go to change and then call a cab. Only when I arrive home do I take a look at the envelope. I breathe a sigh of relief. This is not only enough to pay off all my debts, but also to keep me afloat for a few weeks until I get a job again.

Happily, I let myself fall into my bed. I am so glad that I dared to do it. Not only because I am now finally debt-free again, but also because I have discovered a completely new side of me that I can and will now live out.

Printed in Great Britain
by Amazon